LADY FILMY FERN
or The Voyage of the Window Box

by THOMAS HENNELL

Illustrated by EDWARD BAWDEN

HAMISH HAMILTON · London

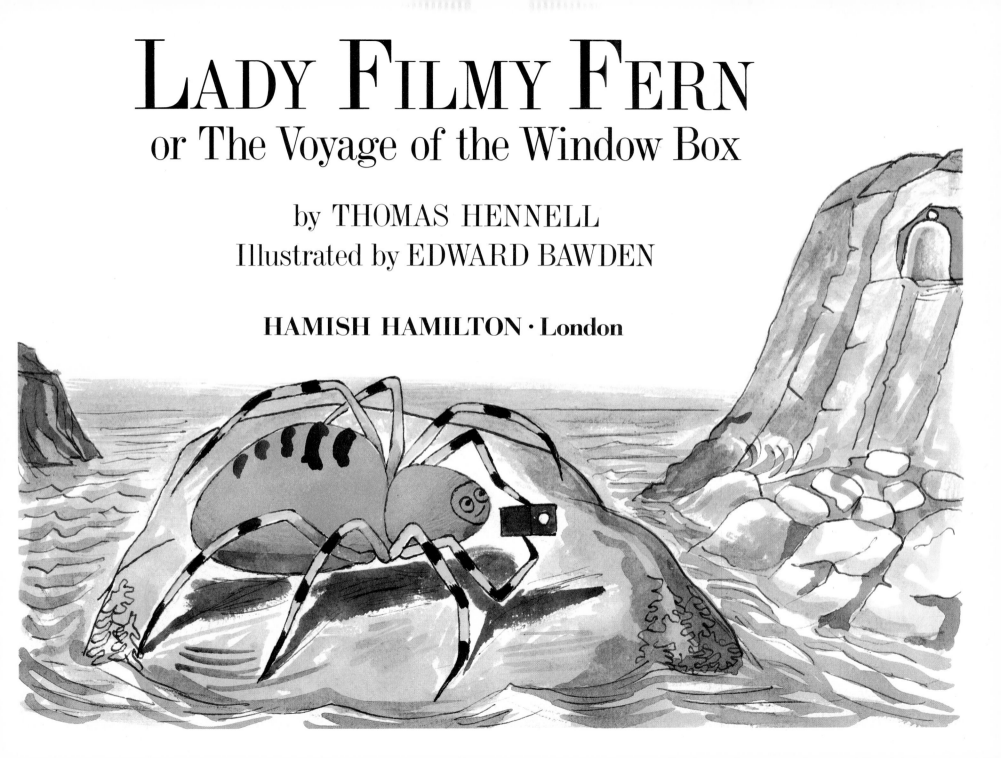

First published in Great Britain 1980
by Hamish Hamilton Ltd
Garden House   57-59 Long Acre   London WC2E 9JZ

Copyright©Edward Bawden, The Hennell Estate,
Peyton Skipwith, Cameron & Tayleur (Books) Ltd, 1980

British Library Cataloguing in Publication Data
Hennell, Thomas
   Lady Filmy Fern
   I. Title   II. Bawden Edward
   823'.9'1J   PZ7.H391/

   ISBN 0-241-10468-8

Produced by Cameron & Tayleur (Books) Ltd
25 Lloyd Baker Street   London WC1X 9AT
Setting by Modern Text Typesetting
16 West Street   Prittlewell   Southend   Essex
Reproduction by Gateway Platemakers Ltd
1 Pardon Street   London EC1V 0AQ
Printed and bound in Italy by LEGO   Vicenza

INTRODUCTION

EDWARD BAWDEN, the principal creator of *Lady Filmy Fern*, and Eric Ravilious met when they were fellow students at the Royal College of Art in Kensington. As an escape from London, they rented half of Brick House in the Essex village of Great Bardfield for the princely sum of 3s 6d a week. It was here that they met Tom Hennell, a fellow artist, who was touring the country gathering material for his first book, *Change in the Farm*. 'One morning in 1931,' Edward Bawden recalled nearly fifty years later, 'when Eric Ravilious and I came down to the kitchen in Brick House to wash ourselves we found a stranger stripped to the waist, pumping water over his head and making quite a splash in the large slate sink. He was tall and thin, with black beady eyes rather close set, dark, slightly curly hair and as he greeted us his voice had a deep, booming parsonic ring, which echoed even more loudly when he laughed. Outside, leaning against the doorpost was a heavy, khaki-coloured Army bike and on it, tied to the bar between the saddle and the steering wheel, a large, perfect specimen of a corn dolly, of the sort known as The Lord's Table. Tom greeted us in the most friendly manner. Our identity was divulged in a matter of seconds and friendship established immediately.' It was a strange meeting, but explained by the fact that Hennell had arrived in Bardfield late the previous evening and had been given a room by their landlady.

The following year, Bawden married Charlotte Epton, and his father bought Brick House for them as a wedding present. Ravilious also married, and, with his wife, Tirzah, continued to spend weekends and holidays at the house. Another regular visitor was Gwyneth Lloyd Thomas, an English don at Girton College, Cambridge. To amuse themselves during the lamp-lit evenings they invented three characters, whose story developed in a manner akin to the game of Consequences; it unfolded intermittently over a period of several months. The characters were Lady Filmy Fern, Mr Virgin Cork and the Welsh Polypod. In order to breathe extra life into these three and to prolong the story-telling, Bawden decided to make drawings of the characters and to illustrate incidents in their adventures. When these watercolour illustrations were shown to Tom Hennell on one of his visits to Bardfield, he willingly participated in the recreation of the tale and was persuaded to write it down. The resulting manuscript, along with Bawden's watercolours, was shown to only one publisher; after a rejection, the illustrations were pasted into a scrapbook, where they remained for the next 45 years.

At the outbreak of war in 1939, Bawden, Hennell and Ravilious offered their services to the War Artists' Commission. When Bawden was sent overseas the following year, he placed much of his work, including the *Lady Filmy Fern* scrapbook, down a well in the garden of Brick House, with the idea that it would be safe there and could be retrieved later, 'after the Germans had retreated.' That the well was none too dry is evident from the rich patina which some of the watercolours still bear, despite the careful attention which has recently been lavished on them by Miss Lewisohn of the Conservation Department of the Fitzwilliam Museum, Cambridge.

Hennell, who had suffered from a serious spell of mental illness during the 1930s, was not appointed an Official War Artist until 1943 when he was invited to 'record aspects of the war in Iceland.' By an ironic twist of fate he was sent there as replacement for Eric Ravilious, who had been reported missing on an air patrol off Iceland in September

1942. Hennell went on to record the preparations in England for D-Day and its aftermath in France. Later he accompanied the Allied Advance in Europe, and was then posted to the Far East attached to the RAF. In November 1945 he was captured by Indonesian nationalists and reported 'missing believed killed.'

Lady Filmy Fern emerged from the well after the War, but continued to lie neglected until the Autumn of 1979, when two exhibitions were being planned which led to her rediscovery. Bawden had sent the watercolours to Miss Lewisohn in preparation for an exhibition of his book illustrations, which I was organising for The Fine Art Society in London. When I saw them, their potential for publication struck me so strongly that, instead of including them in the exhibition and risking their dispersal, I asked Bawden whether a copy of the story still existed. A few days later I received from him Hennell's tattered typescript. At much the same time, Michael Macleod of Goldsmiths' College, London University, was organising an exhibition, *Drawn from Nature*, of work by three friends—Tom Hennell, A.S. Hartrick and Vincent Lines. His interest had been kindled by finding a second typescript of *Lady Filmy Fern*. It was in response to Michael Macleod's enquiries that Bawden set down his recollections of that morning in Brick House in 1931 when he first encountered Tom Hennell; in that same letter he also said 'my wife and I, Eric and Tirzah Ravilious and Gwyneth Lloyd Thomas regarded Tom as being a man of genius. Alas, he barely reached fulfilment of what he might have achieved had his life been prolonged.'

Edward Bawden, now the sole survivor, whilst professing some surprise at the new-found enthusiasm to disinter *Lady Filmy Fern*, has characteristically thrown himself into the idea of publication and made several extra illustrations in order to create the necessary balance of pictures and text.

PEYTON SKIPWITH

Brick House Garden Party, an illustration by Edward Bawden for *Good Food* (Faber & Faber, 1932). Tom Hennell and Eric Ravilious on the left, Edward Bawden and Tirzah Ravilious on the right.

LADY FILMY FERN had gone to live in retirement at Sandy Cove. The reason for this was that she was tired of Society, and disliked photographers. They were always putting snap-shots of her in the newspapers: society beauty opening this or opening that. She was always opening something or other, yet she never had time for the things she most cared about, her garden, her painting and her reading. And though Lady Filmy Fern wished to fulfil her social duties, it grew very tiresome always to be noticed when she had to do sham things, and to lose all the time that she would have spent on painting and gardening with these troublesome interruptions.

So now she lived by the sea, under the bell-glass which served her for a house, on a ledge near the base of precipitous cliffs. Her only visitors were the sea gulls which came to her door to ask for bird-seed. Being a lady of very delicate tastes, she lived on little else and always had enough to spare for these white-winged visitors.

No-one could climb down the cliff, because it was too steep. At the foot of the path to her ledge lived her only neighbour, Mr Virgin Cork, and very few people got past him. He bought bird-seed for Lady Filmy Fern, when she wanted it, from the village stores. Mr Virgin Cork was a carpenter who made garden seats, trellises and gates from the wood that was cast ashore by the tide. At that moment, he was making a window-box for Lady Filmy Fern.

But what horrible creature was this with many legs, which approached from the brow of the cliff, letting itself down by a strong rope? Its eyes were glued to a camera, which it held in its front pair of hands, trying to get the focus for a snap-shot. It was the Welsh Polypod, of all photographers the most resourceful, ambitious and unscrupulous.

Lady Filmy Fern fled in horror, followed by her cat, its fur and tail bristling. The sea gulls dispersed with loud cries of distress and alarm.

But Mr Virgin Cork intercepted the marauder. 'None of that,' he said firmly, 'Not in Sandy Cove. We don't permit strangers.'

The Polypod tried to argue. 'But I'm a regular camera-man, a public character. No lady of distinction, no celebrated actress, or fashionable beauty, who comes within the range of my lens ever fails to be netted. You can't keep me out.'

'We'll see about that,' said Mr Virgin Cork, taking up a large screwdriver. This alarmed the Polypod, who scuttled off with his camera, till he reached a place of safety among the fallen rocks. But every now and then, as he got over his fright, he could be seen furtively glancing out from the crevices to spy upon Lady Filmy Fern, and trying again to focus his lens on her.

'If only I could get her,' he thought, 'I should be better paid for a picture of her in Sandy Cove, where she is such a rarity, than for all the illustrations of her in fashionable circles.'

Lady Filmy Fern had also got over her surprise and alarm, but she was disturbed and offended.

'It is clear,' said she to Mr Virgin Cork, 'nothing less than a sea voyage will rid us of these detestable intruders. Cannot you manage to make some sort of a boat that we could sail away in; to carry us past the reach of inquisitive persons?'

'Certainly, Lady Filmy', answered Mr Virgin Cork readily, 'nothing easier. Let me get to work straight away, and by this evening all shall be ready for the voyage.'

So Mr Virgin Cork rolled up his sleeves and began at once to turn the window-box into a sailing ship. When it was nearly ready, he moved in Lady Filmy Fern's bell glass, her chair and table, some flowers and a portmanteau, not forgetting anything that would be necessary or useful to them. So they were well provisioned for a long time at sea.

In the evening a gentle breeze sprang up, which carried the window-box from Sandy Cove out to sea with the ebbing tide. Some gulls followed them, swooping and loudly beating the air with their wings, crying unhappily, as if to beg them not to go away. But Sandy Cove and its cliffs grew smaller and smaller; the Lady and the Carpenter could see more and more of the length of the coastline as it sank lower and lower, till at last the tallest objects on the shore were seen no more; the church spire dipped below the rim of the ocean, and night came up, covering the dark sea with stars.

The Polypod had watched uneasily as Mr Virgin Cork made his preparations to bear off Lady Filmy Fern; he became distressed as he saw them sailing further and further away in the window-box. He climbed as hastily as he could to the top of the cliff to watch them still further—and he might have been seeing them for the very last time. But just then a gull settled close by him (without noticing him, he kept so very still); quick as thought, the Polypod tied an end of his long rope to one of the gull's legs. Presently, the gull took flight, rising very high into the air, and making southward, in the same direction as that taken by the window-box. So as the sea gull flew swiftly, it began to over-take the boat, and the Polypod (though short-sighted) could make out Mr Virgin Cork and Lady Filmy Fern, under her glass bell, more and more distinctly. He had not forgotten to take his camera with him. But it was growing too dark to use it.

As night advanced, a storm blew up, but though it began to rain, the wind made the window-box sail much faster. Lady Filmy Fern was dry and comfort-able under her glass dome; Mr Virgin Cork opened an umbrella with one hand, while he baled out the boat with a teacup in the other.

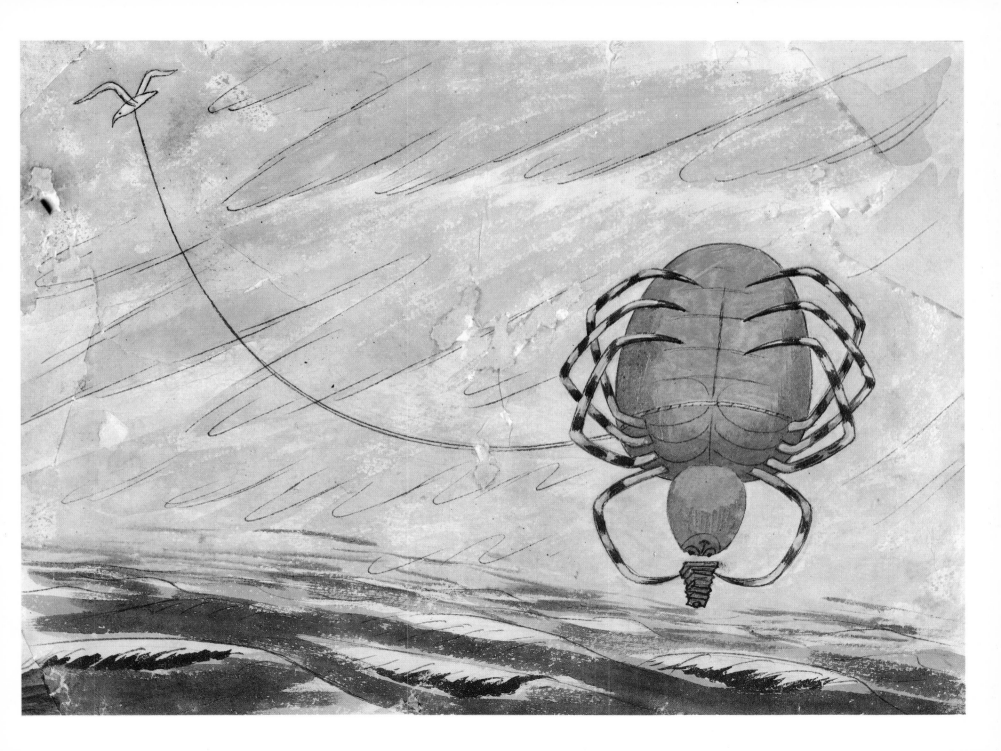

But the sea gull was not getting along nearly so well; it flapped and struggled as the rain beat down on its wings and broad back. The rain made the Polypod wet and heavy, as well as very uncomfortable.

'Whatever can be the matter?' the gull muttered crossly to itself. 'I feel as heavy as if I were carrying a great parcel of luggage. Well, whoever's luggage it may be, it's in for a wetting now, that's all!'

The Polypod was dreadfully frightened on overhearing these words for he could not swim, and there was not a speck of land in sight as far as he could see. But he could think of no way to save himself as the gull dived smoothly down upon the sea and, folding his wings, settled on the waves like a cork.

The Polypod tried frantically to haul in the rope, to climb on the sea gull's back, but the rope was far too long and too heavy. As soon as a little of it was coiled in, Polypod sank and swallowed a great deal of very nasty sea water. He sank several times; the more he struggled to swim, the worse it was; but on coming up for the third or fourth time, he saw a large object floating near at hand. He could not tell what it was, but with his last remaining strength he clambered upon it; and there he rested until he began to feel better. He still clutched his camera.

As it grew lighter towards morning, the Polypod began to see what the thing was that had kept him afloat. It was a large bottle, but an unusual one, for there was something very strange inside it. The rain had ceased, but it still blew a gale; the sea was very rough, and it was some time before the Polypod could make out what was inside the bottle. At last he realised it was a ship with all its masts, spars, and sails set.

'Just the thing,' thought the Polypod 'to sail in pursuit. Expert sailor that I am, I shall soon be able to overhaul the Lady's window-box, and her plodding old landlubber, Virgin Cork.'

It was not at all an easy matter to get this ship out of the bottle; anyone who understood ships less well than the Polypod, might have tried and failed, again and again. But he worked away, and as he worked, he sang this shanty:

> The clouds are all white
> The skies are all bright
> The tackle's all right
> And we're bound for the Bay of Biscay—O.

The Polypod sang very loud, and perhaps not very well; but there was no-one near to criticise. Scarcely had he finished his song, when the ship was free of the bottle and afloat on her own keel, the camera safely stowed for cargo and ballast, and the Polypod was aloft in the rigging, trimming and shortening sail, with all his hands busy.

The day was now brilliant; the ship flew like an arrow through the clear waves, leaving a long wake of white foam behind her.

The window-box travelled on more slowly, but (like the tortoise in its race with the hare) kept going steadily, and met with few hindrances. Mr Virgin Cork had taken care to provide papers and passports that were in order, and he always managed to deal with customs officers or pilots in the very best way, quite polite but decisively, wasting no time. But the Polypod, being rude by nature, was always in trouble. He had no papers or anything to show that he had lawful business at sea. So he often had to run off his course to avoid awkward meetings or to escape coastguards. If he had not been very persistent in following them, Lady Filmy Fern and Mr Virgin Cork might have run away clear of him altogether.

While they were passing through the Mediterranean Sea, Lady Filmy Fern read poetry, under her bell-glass. Mr Virgin Cork smoked his pipe, at his end of the window-box. But he kept a sharp look-out.

So the time passed quickly, and the journey went very pleasantly. When they had left the Greek Islands behind them, they entered the Suez Canal. And here Lady Filmy Fern made drawings of the Pyramids; Virgin Cork played his mouth-organ, which chimed in with the sound of the ripples. The window-box was drawn along by a handsome high-stepping camel, which leaped over the bollards along the tow-path, to which the large ships were hitched up when the water was let in or out of the canal.

And so they travelled through the Suez Canal, into the Red Sea, and thence by the Gulf of Arabia to the Indian Ocean.

They began slowly to travel along the coast between Bombay and Ceylon. They had time to bathe, visit many ports and to see interesting and remarkable sights. It seemed likely that in this way they would travel south-eastward by way of Borneo and the South Seas, and home at last by Cape Horn. This was a long journey, and Lady Filmy Fern sometimes thought about home; she wondered whether, by spending so long in travelling, she could possibly be missing any important enjoyments. Mr Virgin Cork was running short of tobacco; his favourite kind could only be bought in Bristol. So he suggested that they should get a lift for part of the way on board a liner. Lady Filmy Fern agreed, on condition they were protected from photographers.

Meanwhile, what had become of the Polypod? He seemed by now to have given up trying to pursue them. But this was not so. The fact was that he had got into trouble again. He had already been in difficulties with harbour-masters and such people at Gibraltar, at Malta, Minorca, Crete and Cyprus; the authorities were beginning to know him. So when he refused at Port Said to let a pilot come on board and fought with the customs officers, who tried to examine his camera, he had to be forcibly ejected from his ship, which was taken in charge by the Port Admiral. In the end, he only just managed to escape them, or they would have tried him for piracy. But he got away, though the officers had taken his camera from him. He was determined to follow on foot, all the way along the Canal.

But the camel was far ahead, towing the window-box along at a pretty smart rate. The Polypod was still in a furious temper and stalked along, never looking behind him or noticing the weather, but bent on having his revenge. In this way he was overtaken very suddenly by a sandstorm, which, arriving quite unexpectedly, blew him right across the canal, and on, rolling him over and over in the sand, for a great many miles. The Polypod hunched himself up into a ball, but the tighter he hunched himself, the more he was rolled along. So at last he was rolled over the mountains and into Afghanistan.

For some time he managed to live as an assistant to a native juggler, who taught him The Improved Rope Trick. For a time he liked the novelty of this, but when it began to wear off, he realised that a life of independent enterprise and adventure was the only one that could really suit him.

One day a large aeroplane, which was attempting a record flight round the world, settled quite near, and while a crowd of Afghans were talking to the pilot and offering to sell him different things, the Polypod climbed stealthily on board, and hid in a box marked Life-belts. It was very hot and uncomfortable, with nothing to eat or drink but what the Polypod could find when he crept out, very quietly, at night.

'Anyway,' he said to himself, 'it won't be for long. We do a thousand miles a day; and we don't wait about anywhere. Where is the poor old window-box now, I wonder? Ho, Ho!'

It was on the return journey, as the airmen were passing over the Sargasso Sea, that the pilot's companion caught sight of something below that looked like a ship in distress. He called to the pilot, who flew down so that they could get a clearer view. But all they could see was a derelict window-box; on which Lady Filmy Fern and Mr Virgin Cork were standing. She was waving a handkerchief, while he had tied his shirt to the mop and was signalling, as though with a flag.

The pilot's companion ran to get life-belts, but no sooner had he opened the box than out jumped the Polypod from hiding. It was not before they had chased him all around the cabin and on to the wings, that he was able to lower himself overboard and crawl away on the Sargasso weed, while the two airmen were very carefully hauling Lady Filmy Fern and Mr Virgin Cork on board the 'plane. They were hungry and exhausted, but they soon revived, and in a very short time they were both back at home in England, none the worse for their adventures. (Mr Virgin Cork had not had a shave during the whole voyage.)

The window-box had become an almost total wreck, but in spite of that, the Welsh Polypod was able to occupy it and to make it his home. Life in the Sargasso Sea suited his tastes; he found enough victims to enable him to live comfortably. For all I know, he lives there still. When he felt dull, the Polypod used Lady Filmy Fern's bell-glass for deep-sea diving. It may seem unlikely that the Polypod could have done this all by himself, but it was a feat no more difficult, I can assure you, than that of getting the ship out of the bottle.